On Fire

April Alieda

Flower Moon Publishing

Chapter One

♥

C HELSEA DRAKE'S LUNGS BURNED. Scorched by the billowing black smoke and increasing heat. The air smelled of burning plastic and shattered dreams. The sounds of the fire muted the sirens she knew were outside. Her eyes stung and made it nearly impossible to keep them open, but she had to keep going. She had to find him. She couldn't go back out without him. Eli would never recover. She would never get over letting him down again.

"Ma'am, what the heck are you still doing in here? We need to go." A deep male voice that seemed to emanate from the smoke made her jump.

"I'm not leaving Jake." Chelsea still couldn't see the fireman who owned the voice, but she took a step away from him.

"Is there another person in the house?" The voice barked behind her, just as close as when she heard it the first time. It seemed he could see her better than she could see him.

"What? No, the dog." Chelsea took another step taking her deeper into the house, and closer to the heat of the fire.

Maybe if she pulled her shirt over her eyes, she could keep them open for more than a second and look through the fabric for the dog. He had to be okay. She pulled the collar of her shirt to her forehead and took a step forward. She slammed into something hard. *A wall?* She tentatively guided her hand to feel her way around the obstacle, hoping she wouldn't be burned. *Whoa.* She was picked up at the waist, swept her completely off her feet and over what felt like a shoulder. Jesus, he made it seem like she weighed two pounds less than nothing.

"Put me down." Her voice barely audible, even to herself, above the swelling sound of the sirens, plus the fire, and water cascading over the house. He dared to ignore her.

She slapped his back and yelled, "I said put me down." Her voice more insistent. "I need to get Jake."

He didn't say anything but tightened his grip.

She struggled against it but didn't have any effect.

He refused to put her down even when they were outside. Instead, he carried her to the street and set her down on a stretcher by the ambulance. She immediately jumped back up and tried to get passed him so she could get back into the burning house.

He grabbed her and set her back down then lifted his oxygen mask. "Stay there."

She jumped back up. "My son can't lose his dog too, get out of my way."

He caught her, lifted her off the ground, and sat her back onto the stretcher. "Listen to me. Stop. They're both right here."

"Mom!" Eli's voice sounded smaller than usual. He was terrified. That kind of fear shouldn't touch such a young child.

"Eli, I'm okay. Everything's okay." She hoped her voice convinced him because she wasn't sure at all.

"I didn't think...." Eli's little voice trembled and tore at Chelsea's heart. He'd suffered so much over the last year. She couldn't blame him for fearing the worst.

"Shhh. I'm here." Jake put his front paws onto the side of the stretcher and yelped. Chelsea pulled Eli in tight for a hug, she held onto him and rocked a bit. She released her grip on Eli and then patted the dog's head. She looked back at Eli and pulled him in for another hug. What would have she done if something had happened to him? They were covered in soot but otherwise physically okay. Thank goodness they were all safe. Chelsea felt the tears building but swallowed hard to push them back down. She'd have plenty of time to cry later, now was not the time. Not in front of Eli.

"Chelsea, Eli!" Alexandra Cordova's voice cracked as she pushed her daughter, Ashley, in a stroller toward them.

"Oh, Alex." There in her sister's arms, Chelsea began to shake like it was January instead of mid-April.

"Why are you on the stretcher? Are you hurt?" Alex kept her arms around Chelsea, but leaned back and searched her sister's eyes for answers.

"The stupid fireman insisted on putting me on the stretcher. I'm fine, I promise. Eli is too."

"I'm so glad you're both....You just got here. I don't know what I would have done." Alex pulled Chelsea back in, squeezed tighter, and whispered. "Hang on just a bit longer, Eli needs to see you hold it together."

Chelsea nodded against Alex's cheek.

Alex let her sister go and pulled her nephew in for a bear hug.

"Auntie, you're suffocating me." Eli's arms were trapped against his sides, or Chelsea was sure he would have pushed back against his aunt.

"Sorry, not sorry dude." She looked back at Chelsea. "Are they taking you to the hospital?" Alex asked.

"Not if I have anything to say about it. We're fine. The house, not so much. What are we going to do?" Chelsea felt the weight of the situation crush against her chest. She looked at the house that was barely there. The flames danced as if to mock her hope for a better life, with each flash another piece of her already tattered life evaporated before her.

The fire and lights from the emergency equipment lit the sky like it was mid-day. Chelsea shielded her eyes. Half the town gathered across the street. This wasn't exactly how she planned to announce her arrival. She surveyed the scene, the firefighters stood like sentinels around the house, maybe they could save part of it. As if on cue the roof above what would have been Eli's room collapsed. Chelsea's shoulder's slumped, and her chin hit her chest.

Alex reached over and squeezed Chelsea's shoulder. "Let's get you to Magnolia. We'll worry about the rest in the morning, over an Irish coffee." Alex smiled, but it lacked its usual lightness. At that moment Chelsea didn't know much, but she did know it was going to take more than one cup of Irish coffee to fix this.

Chapter Two

♥

"**Y**OU'RE GOING TO BE late for your first practice Eli, let's go!" Chelsea yelled into the kitchen at Magnolia Inn.

"Coming!" Eli called back, then ran through the swinging door into the parlor.

"Are you excited?" Chelsea asked as she put her arm around his shoulder and pulled him in for a squeeze.

"Nah, it's just baseball."

Chelsea stole a glance at her son. "You love baseball."

"I loved watching baseball with my friends." He pulled back from her hug.

"You'll make new friends." She bumped his shoulder with the side of her fist.

Eli shrugged. "Sure."

"Hey, we talked about this before we moved." They both can't have second thoughts at the same time.

"I know. It's just. I mean. What if I'm not any good?" Eli didn't look at her.

"You'll be great, no worries." Chelsea ruffled his hair with her hand.

"Easy for you to say." Eli mumbled.

"Seriously dude, it'll be okay."

"Sure."

They rushed to the school and made it to the park just as the coach called the boys to the field. Eli looked tiny next to the other kids. Good thing this wasn't football. Chelsea joined the other moms on the bleachers. They seemed to be entrenched in their own conversations and didn't notice her which worked for Chelsea. Eli wasn't the only one concerned about making new friends because of their move.

The coach seemed familiar, had she met him at Alexandra and Duncan's wedding? He towered over the boys. His arms looked larger than Eli's waist, damn they were huge. He reached out and ruffled Eli's hair. His smile...

"Keep looking at Coach like that, and no one will talk to you." Alex's familiar voice broke into her thoughts like a thief.

"I'm sorry, what?" Chelsea tried without much success to escape the fog that settled around her when she saw him.

"Mick's the most eligible bachelor in town these days. The other mothers won't take to kindly if you swoop in and steal him away." Alex offered.

"I don't know what you're talking about. I didn't know you were coming out, I could have given you a ride."

"You're almost as good as mom in changing the subject, kudos." Alex grinned.

"I don't know what you're talking about. I just feel guilty because you walked."

"Don't worry about it. Ashley wanted a walk and we just kind of ended up here. How's Eli making out?"

"They haven't done anything yet, just talking."

"Oh. Here they go." Alex pointed to the field.

They split into two groups. Eli followed Coach's group. Chelsea watched them do drills, throwing and catching the ball. Chelsea held her breath. "Alex, what are we going to do? Eli is dropping ball after ball, and he can't throw more than a few feet."

"I'm sure he'll be fine." Alex tried to assure her.

"I want to be angry with Mark, but even if he were still alive, he didn't spend enough time with his son to make a difference."

"It's not like he was an athlete. I don't think it would have mattered how much time they spent together, they wouldn't have played base-ball. Sports weren't exactly Mark's thing."

"True, but sports aren't exactly my thing either, like seriously not my thing." Chelsea sighed. "I guess that needs to change."

"Or you could let Coach, coach. It doesn't look like the other boys are giving him a hard time."

"Thank goodness for small miracles."

Ashley began to fuss in her stroller. "Well, I guess the princess has had enough of the outdoors. See you in a bit back at the inn?"

"Yes, I don't think we'll be much longer." Chelsea watched as Alex and Ashley walked back toward the inn.

Coach's voice caught her attention, she turned back to the field and watched him interact with the boys. *Most eligible bachelor?* Not that it mattered. She may be single, but she's far from available. Eli was her focus. He was the most important person in her life. She didn't have time to get lost in those rugged, muscular arms no matter how inviting they were. Not to mention that smile that could make a girl forget....Wait, why is his killer smile getting closer? Retreat. Retreat. Chelsea couldn't escape, the other moms surrounded her, seemingly wanting to get closer to his smile.

"Did you see me, mom?" Eli's voice, from his spot next to Coach, broke through her panic.

"Sure did." The mom in front of her stepped aside so Chelsea could step down from the bleachers.

"Coach says I need practice."

Chelsea's eyes narrowed and she wished they could throw actual lawn darts at Coach. His smile dimmed for a millisecond.

"We can make that happen," Chelsea reassured Eli.

"Why don't you join the other guys, looks like they're raiding the snacks." Coach pointed Eli to the bench on the other side of home plate.

That voice. Chelsea had met him before, but where? How could she possibly forget him, he's darn near unforgettable.

Eli looked at Chelsea for confirmation it was okay, she nodded, and Eli ran off.

Chelsea folded her arms against herself and watched Eli. She couldn't focus so she wouldn't have been able to tell you what he or the other guys around him were doing, but at least she wasn't looking at Coach.

"So, um. This is unexpected." Coach offered.

"Unexpected?" Chelsea couldn't hide her confusion.

"Anastasia is a small town since I hadn't seen you around since that night, I figured you decided to leave."

"That night? What are you...oh." Chelsea realized who he was. She took a step back. She needed air. She immediately regretted not being one of those moms who came to practice looking like they were about to go to dinner with the royal family. No, her look was more Wal-Mart after a bender.

"Like I said, unexpected." He flashed a smile that could have ignited an icicle.

Don't look directly at him. "Is it really though? He is ten, and this is the only team for his age." Chelsea's tone was sharp. It always was when she was stressed.

"Well, I guess when you put it that way."

"Mm-hmm." Chelsea could see him shifting beside her.

He reached into his back pocket and pulled out his wallet. "We didn't officially meet, I'm Mick Wilson, Anastasia's fire captain. Here's my card, in case you'd like to call me."

Chelsea didn't move.

"Ya know so that I can help Eli."

"Help Eli?" Chelsea raised an eyebrow.

"Practice. He seems behind the others."

"I don't need your card. I'll help my son."

"You can play?"

"Of course I can play. Ever heard of softball?" She might not have ever played, but no way she'd admit that to him.

"Funny. Maybe take my card as a backup?" Mick held the card up again toward her hand.

"No thanks. Eli, time to go." Chelsea signaled to Eli, waving him toward her.

"I could look at the roster, but could I get your name?"

There's that damn smile again.

"Please."

"Chelsea. Chelsea Drake."

"Nice to officially meet you, Chelsea."

Chelsea forced a fake smile as Eli arrived at her side and they walked toward their car. Eli looked back at Coach and waved.

Maybe there's a team in Whatsell. That's it. She'd just find him another team. *How hard could it be?*

Mick watched them walk away. *What just happened?* No one had ever turned down his number. He waited for the other families to clear from practice, gathered the equipment, and walked toward Main Street. Practice always made him hungry.

The bell chimed when Mick opened the screen door to Flower Moon Café. It was mid-afternoon, so the lunch crowd was gone, but the dinner rush hadn't started yet.

"Perfect timin'. Toby's just puttin' the last dish into yer order." Miss Sadie offered from behind the counter.

"Terrific. Thanks, Miss Sadie."

Miss Sadie nodded. "Do ya have time for coffee and pie?"

Mick shrugged. "Will you be joining me?"

"I don't see why not."

"Then, I'd love some." Mick smiled.

"You are too much, ya know that?"

"I might have been told that a time or two."

Miss Sadie laughed, grabbed them each a slice of pie, poured two cups of coffee and then pointed to one of the booths against the wall.

"How's yer mama makin' out in Atlanta?"

"Chompin' at the bit to get back to Anastasia." Mick sat in the booth, opened the napkin roll and placed the napkin over his lap.

"I bet that's right. How's Tamika doin'?" Miss Sadie set the food on the table and slid into the booth across from Mick.

"More anxious than mama." Mick laughed.

Miss Sadie joined in the laughter. "I don't doubt that either. What are the doctors sayin'?"

"She should be back in town raising Cain before school's out."

"Don't that beat all. Glad to hear it. I figured a few weeks with the grandbabies, and she'd be right as rain." Miss Sadie nodded and took a sip of her coffee.

"From your lips to God's ears Miss Sadie. I'm not ready for her to be gone." Mick shook his head.

"And ya never will be. Now, what's this mischief I hear ya have planned with Duncan next weekend?"

"What makes you think it's mischief?" Mick smirked.

"Cuz I know ya boys better than ya know yerselves."

"Not this time." Mick winked at Miss Sadie. "We're organizing a community service drive for veterans. Putting together groups to mow lawns, paint houses, make minor repairs, that kind of thing. The Girl Scouts are putting together care packages with toothpaste and toothbrushes, razors, deodorant, combs, feminine hygiene products to hand out. We hope it's enough of a success that we can make the day an annual event or maybe even a twice a year thing."

"Sounds nice but if I had money to bet, mischief would find ya one way or another." Miss Sadie grinned.

Mick nodded. "Guess I can't argue much with that."

"Enough talkin', take a bite of that pie. I need to know what ya think. I'm tryin' a new recipe."

Mick took a bite, and his tongue burned a bit. "That's got a kick to it." Mick took another taste and then a sip of his coffee.

"Too much?"

"No, it's strong but good. It makes itself known and then fades. I like it. What is it?"

"Good question. I'm not sure what I want to call it yet."

"Well if I think of something, I'll let you know."

"Do ya think Oatmeal Cinnamon is too obvious?" Miss Sadie asked, an uncharacteristic hesitance in her voice.

"What's wrong with obvious? I think it is perfect. The crust tastes like an oatmeal cookie, and the cinnamon in the filling gets your attention."

"No need to make it complicated, I guess."

"Exactly." Mick took another bite of pie and smiled.

Toby came out of the kitchen with two large bags that seemed to be busting at the seams. "Hey Mick, your orders ready."

"Thanks, Toby. Miss Sadie's not working you too hard is she?"

"Every day." Toby grinned.

"Hey now." Miss Sadie flicked her fork toward Toby.

Toby threw his arms up and turned toward the kitchen. "Catch ya later Mick."

"See ya Toby."

"Stay out of trouble." Miss Sadie called to Mick.

Mick looked back over his shoulder and winked. "Not likely."

Chapter Three

♥

CHELSEA STOOD IN MAGNOLIA Inn's kitchen chugging a glass of water. She looked over the rim of the glass at the baseball glove she'd set on the counter and couldn't shake the feeling it mocked her. She had helped Eli for a couple of weeks now, but she doubted anyone could tell. He maybe caught one or two more balls than he had when they started but given the amount of time they'd spent he really should have been better. Had she finally met her match, was baseball the one thing she couldn't conquer? Why did she pretend she played softball when Mick asked? Well, because she wasn't about to admit to him, she couldn't play.

Chelsea looked at her watch. How was it time for his regular practice already? Chelsea drank another glass of water and then headed to the bottom of the stairs. "Eli, time for practice," Chelsea called up the stairs.

"Do we have to?" Eli whined from somewhere on the second floor, near the top of the stairs.

"Yep. We're not quitters. We need to see this through."

Eli trudged down the stairs, stopped at the landing, and looked down at her. "I know that here." Eli pointed to his head. "But here is tired." He pointed to his heart.

"I understand. The season is almost over. We can do it, I promise."

Eli nodded, bounded down the stairs, Chelsea stopped him, and hugged him.

When they stepped outside Chelsea realized her car was blocked in by other guests. She considered going back into the inn to find the guests but instead, turned to Eli. "How about we walk to the field?"

Eli shrugged, "Sure."

"Oof, hold down that enthusiasm." Chelsea wrapped her arm around Eli and pulled him toward her.

Eli struggles against her, "Funny mom, now let me go before someone sees."

Chelsea squeezed his shoulder with her hand, but then let him go not sure if she was ready for Eli to not need her so much. Funny how that works, she spent his toddler years wishing he could fend for himself a bit more, but as he became more independent, she oddly longed for those needier years to come back. As they walked along Chelsea didn't see anyone she knew. Small-town life was strange like that, some days she couldn't take two steps without running into someone she know, and yet on other days, she could be out and not see anyone she knew. She'd found the likelihood of running into someone you know was directly proportional to how much she looked like a hot mess. The more of a mess the more people she'll see, it never failed.

Eli seemed quieter than usual, so Chelsea tried to do a quick check-in. "I haven't heard from your teachers lately, how are things going at school?"

"It's so easy mom, well in social studies anyway. They are just talking about Egypt which I did last year. Math, let's not talk about math."

"You are too much like your mother." Chelsea teased. "If you think you need help with the math let me know, I'm sure we could find a tutor."

"Ew."

Chelsea pushed Eli's shoulder and they both laughed. They arrived at the field just in time for Coach to call the boys to the field. Chelsea watched as he ran to join his teammates. He looked like he forgot about not wanting to come to practice, and that he was having fun. At the end of the day, that's all that mattered to Chelsea.

Mick had set up a few drill stations around the field and rotated each group through until the sun disappeared behind the trees on the edges of the outfield. "Okay guys, let's huddle up."

Mick watched as the boys ran toward him, they were quite a group. "You all did well today, keep practicing at home. Next practice we have will be a mock game. Team dismissed. Eli, could you stay for a minute."

"Ohhhhhh." Eli's teammates howled.

"That's enough guys, see you Thursday." Mick scolded and then turned to Eli. "Hasn't your mom helped you practice?"

"Coach, can you keep a secret?" Eli's nose scrunched.

"Most of the time." Mick smiled.

"Mom is worse than me at this baseball thing." Eli's head flopped forward, and he kicked at the ground under his foot.

"Is that right?"

Eli glanced up, and paused before admitting, "Yep."

It was nice to see it pained Eli a little to admit Chelsea wasn't quite cutting it. "That's too bad. I'm sure she's great at other things."

Eli shook his head and looked at the group of teammates who were already eating snacks. He shrugged and said, "she is, and she tried."

"Maybe I can help?"

Eli's head snapped toward Mick. "Really?"

"Sure."

"That'd be great. Let me tell my mom."

Mick tried to stop him, but Eli was too fast. He followed. This would be painful. Dreadfully painful. She had already said no once. He approached and watched as Chelsea's body language went from relaxed to tense in less than a breath. Not happy was an understatement.

Mick didn't hear what was said in the first exchange.

"Right Coach?" Eli asked.

"Sorry, I missed that Eli." Mick looked at Eli but Chelsea spoke.

"I said, isn't that great?" Chelsea said.

When Mick looked at her, everything but the words screamed the opposite.

"What? Oh, yes, it's great. Are you sure?" Mick asked.

"I said it was didn't I?" Chelsea gritted through her teeth.

"I knew you'd be okay with it." Eli hugged Chelsea.

"Are you sure you have time Coach?" Chelsea asked and then leaned her head slowly forward while widening her eyes.

Mick smirked, she seemed to be trying to wiggle her way out of the acceptance of the help. Not on his watch. "I'm sure."

"Great," Chelsea mumbled with more air than sound.

Mick nodded, turned back toward the field, and Eli followed. Hopefully, they will be able to convince her it wasn't such a bad idea.

The next evening Mick met Chelsea and Eli at the baseball field for Eli's first one on one practice. At the same time that Mick directed Eli in drills, he kept an eye on Chelsea. Mick had hoped for an opportunity to spend more time with her while coaching Eli. He liked to think he was a good guy but he wasn't entirely free of ulterior motives.

"Eli, do you think we can convince your mom to join us?" Mick nodded toward Chelsea.

"I doubt it, Coach. She doesn't like to be embarrassed and like I said before, the way she plays. Yikes." Eli shook his head. His voice implied he was an expert compared to her.

Mick had to stifle a laugh. "Maybe we won't mention how bad she is."

"You can try, but it's pretty hard to miss."

Mick nodded. "I think we'll have better luck of her joining us if you ask her."

Eli smiled, ran over to Chelsea, grabbed her hand. Mick could tell Chelsea resisted, but Eli wasn't taking no for an answer. Good kid.

"I can't join the two of you, I didn't even bring my glove," Chelsea explained when Eli got her to the pitcher's mound where Mick stood.

"That's not a problem, I have one here that should work for you." Mick reached down and into an equipment bag that lay next to him. "Here you go."

Chelsea took it. "Gee thanks."

"If I can do it, you can do it, mom." Eli encouraged.

"Thanks. Where do you want me, Coach?" Chelsea asked.

Mick had a thought he couldn't share with Eli there. "Why don't I pitch to you and Eli can go to right field for now. Once you hit a few the two of you can switch places."

"Great," Chelsea replied without a hint of happiness or excitement in her voice.

She grabbed a bat and stood at home plate. Mick pitched, Chelsea swung the bat like an axe, and missed the ball by a mile.

"That's okay, let's try again." Mick took another ball from the basket next to him and tossed it to Chelsea.

Chelsea swung and missed.

Mick looked at the way Chelsea stood with the bat. "I think you should switch your hands."

Chelsea moved her hands but didn't switch them.

Mick jogged toward Chelsea. "Here let me show you."

Chelsea held out the bat.

"You keep it. Stand like I'm about to pitch." Mick waited for Chelsea to reposition herself. When she was finished he wrapped his arms around her and placed her right hand over her left hand on the bat. The way she curved into his body, *concentrate*, "Let me help you do a couple of swings, like this." Mick placed his hands on top of hers and swung the bat with her, to help her to get a feel for how it should go. He didn't want to let her go, but holding her like that much longer would tease the limits of respectability.

When Mick took a step back he could have sworn that Chelsea's body moved with him, as if she didn't want him to put space between them any more than he wanted to put it there.

"Better?" Mick asked.

"What? Oh, um, yes. Thanks." Chelsea stumbled through her words.

Mick walked back to the pitcher's mound and called to Eli "Okay bud, heads up your mom's gonna hit a home run."

Eli didn't say anything but punched his baseball glove twice.

Mick turned toward home plate and pitched to Chelsea.

Chelsea swung and hit the ball but it went straight up into the air. She screamed, dropped the bat, and covered her head with her arms. The ball hit the ground a few feet from Chelsea and she uncovered her head.

"I think that's probably good, would you like to switch places with Eli?"

Chelsea nodded, grabbed the glove, and headed to right field. "Good luck Eli."

"Thanks mom."

Mick waited for Chelsea to get into place and then pitched to Eli. Eli hit the ball decently, but it went straight to Mick. He caught it and pitched again. Eli swung a little too soon that time.

"It's okay, keep your eye on the ball. Let's try again."

"Sure thing Coach." Eli reset and stared at Mick with intense concentration.

The kid should get a trophy for not giving up, even if he wasn't getting better. Mick pitched again, and Eli clipped it. The ball didn't go far, so Mick ran over and scooped it up.

"Better. Let's keep going, okay?" Mick asked.

"Yes, Coach." Eli nodded.

Mick glanced over his shoulder at Chelsea. She wouldn't look at him, her eyes focused on Eli. Had he ever met someone so stubborn? He turned his attention back to Eli and pitched.

Eli connected this time, a solid hit.

Mick turned and ran toward the outfield. He should have let Chelsea get that one, but she was in left, not right field. No reason for her to run the length of the field.

Bam!

Chelsea hit him from the side and their feet tangled. Oh shit. They were going to go down. Turn, turn, turn. He landed, with a thud, on the ground. Chelsea fell on top of him. He didn't move. She hadn't knocked the air out of him, but he was stunned a bit. She must have run full speed toward the ball. He didn't move, her laying on him felt more right that he cared to admit.

"Mom, get off him. You're squishing him!" Eli's voice broke the silence that had fallen on the field.

"I'm so sorry." Chelsea tried to remove herself but couldn't. "A little help?"

"I'm helping as little as possible." Mick grinned, put his hands at her waist and easily lifted her, and set her on the ground next to him.

"You're impossible." Chelsea smacked his shoulder.

"Ouch." Mick rubbed his shoulder.

"That didn't hurt." Chelsea tilted her head, the give me a break implied.

"Wanna bet." Mick smiled and winked at her.

"Time to go Eli." Chelsea stood, smoothed her shirt, and brushed grass from her shorts.

"You don't have to leave," Mick responded.

"Yes, we do." Chelsea's voice held little room for negotiation.

"Aw, mom." Eli moaned.

"We've taken enough of Mi...Coach's time and you've got home-work." The slim margin of flexibility was now completely void from her voice.

Eli sighed. "I guess, thanks for trying to help Coach."

"You bet. Anytime Eli. Chelsea, I'm sorry I wasn't paying attention to where I was going. I hope I didn't make you uncomfortable."

There wasn't any hint of sarcasm or joking in Mick's voice. Chelsea nodded. "I'm sorry too." Mick watched as they walked back to their car and saw Chelsea rest her head against the steering wheel. He'd give almost anything to know what she was thinking. One thing was for sure, she was trouble with a capital T.

Chapter Four

♥

C HELSEA HADN'T SEEN MICK since the mishap at the ballfield where she'd landed directly on top of him. She wasn't ready to face him, she needed more time to clear her mind. One of the perks of living with her sister is that Alex might be willing to help.

"Can I ask a favor?" Chelsea asked.

"Maybe." Alex glanced up from the newspaper she was reading.

"Gee thanks." Chelsea put her hand on her hip.

"What? It's all your fault, sis. I learned a long time ago to be cautious when it comes to favors for you." Alex folded her arms against her body.

"I just need you to take Eli to practice." Chelsea hoped she sounded nonchalant, but she was desperate to avoid baseball. That's not true. She was desperate to avoid Mick. She couldn't handle seeing him. Her ego had taken enough of a beating over the last few months, it couldn't take much more.

"Little league?" Alex asked.

"Yes. What other practice does he have?" Her voice cracked. So much for indifferent.

"Um, not sure. Why is it that you need me to take him?" Alex raised an eyebrow.

How does she even do that? Raise one eyebrow the, freak. "Why?"

"This is going to take forever if you keep repeating me." Alex picked up a pen and began to tap it against the desk.

"I need to run a few errands." Errands that will keep a few miles between arms as big as a house and her.

"Errands? Jiminy Christmas, Chelsea. You need to learn to lie better, seriously! I swear I was a better example when we were kids. Didn't you pay attention?" Alex shook her head.

"Don't care what you believe as long as you do it." Chelsea smiled, but it was fake with a capital f.

Alex dropped the pen onto the top of the desk. "You can't avoid him forever, you know that right?"

"Wanna bet?"

Panic. Chelsea hadn't felt this kind of fear in her entire life, and now in less than six months terror had struck twice. Moving to Anastasia was supposed to make things better. Well, make things easier anyway. Finding out jerk of jerks had a girlfriend was a Caribbean vacation compared to her life since moving. How is that even possible? She parked, probably in a marked space, but maybe not. She'd deal with that later. How could he....

She almost pushed open the automatic doors instead of waiting for them to open. "Where is my son?" Chelsea shrieked at the clerk at the desk just inside the door.

"Ma'am." The woman behind the desk said, ma'am, like she'd been in the job about ten years too long.

"My son, where? I need to find him." The pitch of her voice was so high she barely recognized it.

"Who is your son?" The woman sighed and didn't make eye contact.

"What? My son!"

The clerk finally looked up at her, but her expression showed she wasn't amused. "I got that. What's his name?"

"Oh, sorry. Eli Drake." Chelsea's shoulders dropped.

"They've already taken him back. I'll call Nurse Spry, she'll come to escort you back."

"Can't you just...."

"No." The woman picked up the phone and tilted her head toward Chelsea as if to say go ahead and try it.

Chelsea nodded and began to pace. A terrible mother. THE worst. Never should have had Alex take him to practice, this is all her fault.

The doors to the left of the desk opened and a woman in her mid-fifties with short blond hair and attitude of don't even think of giving me a hard time emerged.

"Mrs. Drake?"

Chelsea nodded, her brain couldn't formulate words, she just wanted to see her son.

"This way."

The nurse was interrupted while escorting Chelsea to Eli. She pointed to a curtain, "Sorry, I'm going to have to deal with this, your son is in there."

Chelsea nodded and took a step toward the curtain. Just as she reached up to move the curtain, she heard Mick and Eli's voices. She couldn't explain it, but she paused, instead of pulling the curtain back.

Mick's voice sounded muffled, but she could just make it out. "What do you think your mom's going to say?"

"Don't worry Coach, I'll protect you." Eli had a serious tone, much older than his age should permit.

Mick chuckled, then asked, "That bad?"

"That bad. She's gonna go crazy mom on you. She can't help it. She loves me."

When did he grow up? Chelsea rubbed her forehead with her hand.

"You've got that right, she does love you, but I think I'll let her take a couple of swings. It'll make her feel better."

"If you say so Coach, but you're going to have to be brave."

Mick laughed louder this time, and Chelsea's heart skipped a few too many beats. Even if Mick drove her crazy, Chelsea couldn't deny he was great with Eli. She couldn't believe he sat with him until she got to the hospital. Duncan was about the only other man Chelsea knew that might have stayed with her son in his moment of crisis. Maybe he wasn't as bad as she thought.

Back in Anastasia, Ricette di Amore, Ric for short, appeared on the island in the kitchen while Miss Sadie mixed a batch of shepherd's pie for the dinner special.

"Well, it's a good thing ya didn't wait much longer. Toby will be along, then ya'd have to wait, and ya'd be keeping me up half the night." Miss Sadie scolded the book.

The book vibrated on the island.

"One minute, let me put this in the oven." Miss Sadie shuffled the pan of shepherd's pie to the oven. She set the timer, then turned back to the island, and removed her necklace as she approached Ric.

Her empty hand brushed against the heart-shaped lock and then she used the key to open the recipe book. Miss Sadie took a step back and let Rick work his magic. Ric's pages fluttered and flipped back and forth until it settled on just the right page. The page erupted in flashes of red, yellow, and orange which seemed fitting seeing as how the pie was for Mick. It was for Chelsea too, but her aura was a bit more subdued than Mick's. Miss Sadie could tell by Chelsea's aura that her life hadn't gone the way she'd expected. Hopefully, though the pie would help change that, even if just a little.

That's all they usually really needed after all. People, whether they like to admit it or not, have a predisposition for love. Light has an advantage over dark. Light doesn't always win, but Miss Sadie would always bet on the light. Always.

Miss Sadie looked at the page before her, unlike the first time Ric had provided the recipe there was a title at the top. Apparently, Ric approved of the simple, straightforward Oatmeal Cinnamon title. Guess there is a first time for everything, as she couldn't recall the last time he'd agreed with her about anything. Ric slammed shut and then reopened to the recipe.

"Get out of my head, ya know I don't like it when ya do that." Miss Sadie admonished.

Ric curved the edges of the pages into the center of the book as if to acknowledge her request.

"Mm-hmm." Miss Sadie made her way to the cabinet, knocked three times, and then opened both doors.

Sitting pretty as a picture on the center shelf were the tools passed down to her. They included the mixing bowl that was blue and purple with silver specs. After all the years that had passed since she first laid eyes on it, she still loved how much it reminded her of the galaxy. A woman could get lost gazing at the seemingly ever-changing mixture of the night sky.

Next to the bowl lay Desi, the golden arrow. This pairing must be more important than Miss Sadie initially realized. First Ric agreed with her about the name of the recipe, and now Desi was where she was supposed to be when she was supposed to be there. Next to Desi lay the wooden spoon carved from an olive tree. Seeing them is like reuniting with old friends.

Miss Sadie removed all three items and placed them next to Ric on the island. She returned to the cabinet, closed the doors, and then tapped twice before reopening the doors. This time, inside the cabinet Miss Sadie found all the ingredients she needed to make the pie. Once she completed two trips from the cabinet to the island, she was ready to begin mixing.

"We don't have a lot of time to get this done Y'all. Let's turn the radio on, maybe it'll help us keep up the pace." Miss Sadie walked to the radio, which was under the window, and turned it on. Lady Gaga's unmistakable voice projected from the speakers, and Miss Sadie sashayed back to the island.

Thirty minutes later, Miss Sadie tapped Desi on the side of the bowl and watched as the gold sparkles landed into the batter. She mixed one last time and then filled the oatmeal crust. In a stroke of perfect timing, Miss Sadie removed the dinner special from the oven and put the oatmeal cinnamon pie in its place.

Once the pie cooled, Miss Sadie wrapped the oatmeal cinnamon pie, placed it in a to-go box, and tied a ribbon around it. She'd be needing it before the end of the day, now if she could keep Toby from giving it away before Mick or Chelsea arrived to pick it up.

Miss Sadie wasn't quite sure which one it'd be, her gift didn't work like that. It was more like a forecast, which is one of the reasons why she didn't share it with many. Spill the beans, and they'd expect her to be able to tell them specifics. Secrets are easier. She placed the scissors she'd used to cut the ribbon back in the cabinet and stopped to touch the keychain in the drawer. Ellie's. Now and then the universe would be sure to remind Miss Sadie of the emptiness, not that she needed reminding. It had been there since the day Ellie left, and if anything the hole in Miss Sadie's heart continued to grow rather than shrink.

Almost two years passed since Ric reemerged. She'd been a fool thinking that his reappearance might signal Ellie's return as well. A damn shame really, how she missed her.

Ting-ting-ting.

The chime from the dining room caught Miss Sadie's attention, and she made her way into the café from the kitchen.

"Chelsea, what a pleasant surprise." Miss Sadie smiled and opened her arms for a hug.

Chelsea accepted the hug and sighed.

"That bad dear?"

"It's just been a tough few months. Eli got hurt at baseball practice, and I wasn't there. Mick Wilson had to take him to the hospital."

"Oh, no. How's Eli now?"

"He'll be okay, in a few weeks, after his arm heals. Poor kid. I haven't figured out how I'm going to make it up to him that I wasn't there, but I thought maybe one of your pies might help me smooth things over with Coach. I feel terrible I wasn't there."

"Mick is accustomed to taking care of things in an emergency, I'm sure he didn't mind."

"Probably true, but it would make me feel better if I said thank you, and I'm sorry without having to say the actual words."

"I'll make ya a deal, ya promise to say the words and I've got just the pie for ya to take to him."

Chelsea took a deep breath and exhaled. "You're right. I promise."

"That's my girl." Miss Sadie reached into the refrigerator under the counter, took out the already boxed pie, and then walked to the register. "Who knows, maybe he'll even share."

Chapter Five

CHELSEA LEFT FLOWER MOON Café and headed straight to Mick's house. If she tried to do anything else first, she would have chickened out for sure.

Chelsea approached Mick's house

Lifted her hand to knock

Lowered her hand.

Lifted her hand to knock

The door opened, and a shirtless Mick stood in the doorway.

"Oh, um, hi. I, uh, here. A peace offering and as a thank you for taking care of Eli." Chelsea thrust the box toward Mick.

Mick took the box from her. "Thank you. Completely unnecessary, but thanks. Come in and have a piece?"

His voice purred somewhere between a Vin Diesel gravel and a Barry White bass.

"Thanks, but I really, um. Sure. That'd be great."

Mick stepped aside and motioned for her to enter.

Chelsea entered but wasn't sure what to do after that so she just stood there and wondered why she'd agreed to have a slice of pie with him.

"The kitchen is straight back." Mick pointed toward the back of the house and then made his way into the kitchen.

Chelsea followed and took the time to admire his back muscles. The man was a freaking God. A freaking God who needed to put a shirt on like five minutes ago.

"Have a seat. I'll be right back." Mick placed the box onto the kitchen island and then disappeared back down the hall.

Chelsea sat on one of the stools at the kitchen island and took a deep breath. Her heart felt like a jackrabbit on speed. Have a piece of pie so as not to be rude, then get out of dodge. Simple, easy, and uncomplicated.

"Sorry, I just got out of the shower." Mick walked toward the island, pulling a t-shirt over his torso.

Chelsea pictured water cascading down Mick's bare chest and followed the flow of the water down. Down too far. *Pull yourself together, for goodness sake you aren't a teenager.*

"Can I offer you a cup of coffee to go with the pie?" Mick at least had the decency to pretend he hadn't noticed her lingering gaze.

"Yes, thank you."

Mick turned toward the Keurig, "Have you had any luck in finding a new house?"

"Not really. I planned to rent for a year, to be sure things would work. In theory, I thought I'd like living close to my sister, but sometimes reality is different."

"I think I understand, although I can't imagine living somewhere else. My sister left town as soon as she could, Anastasia was too small for her. Atlanta suits her well." Mick handed Chelsea her coffee and then placed milk and sugar on the island.

Chelsea nodded. "Alex and I grew up moving around a lot, so I don't know the feeling of having a specific location being home. I think that's helped me as an adult, but the older I get, the more I'd like to find a place to stay if not for me, for Eli."

"You said you planned to rent, have you decided to buy?" Mick pulled plates from one of the cabinets and silverware from one of the drawers.

"I haven't reached out to Hannah yet, but since we've survived living with Alex this long my initial fears of reality not meeting my expectations have passed." Chelsea untied the ribbon from the box and pushed it toward Mick.

Mick opened it and retrieved the pie. "Have you had this pie before?"

"Don't think so."

"Then you are in for a treat. It's one of Miss Sadie's new creations. Oatmeal cinnamon."

"Well, I haven't met a slice of Miss Sadie's pie I haven't liked yet. I doubt that'll be my first."

"Could I ask you a question? If you don't want to talk about it I understand, but I've been curious and I like to get my information from the source."

"I guess." Chelsea wasn't sure she'd want to answer, but she'd at least let him ask.

"Where's Eli's dad?"

"That's easy, he's dead." Chelsea sipped her coffee as if she had just said he was at the grocery store.

"So, you're a widow?" Mick paused the cutting of the pie.

Chelsea shook her head, "No, we had just gone through a divorce. A messy, complicated, life-shattering, divorce."

"Not your idea then?"

"Oh, it was one hundred percent my idea. There wasn't enough room in our house for his girlfriend."

"I see." Mick pulled two slices of pie, placed each on their own plate, and handed Chelsea one of them.

"Not sure that you do, this is how I've explained my feelings to others and the explanation still holds. With the exception of the birth of Eli, that woman was the best thing to ever happen to me."

"Really?"

"I was in a loveless marriage but didn't realize it. She saved me from that. He was a jerk about the whole thing but that had nothing to do with her. Eli and I have had a lot of fun, I mean you know about some of the not fun parts, but we've been able to go places and do things we never could have done if his father was around. It was a blessing, I'm sure he's not looking at it that way from the other side." Chelsea laughed.

"No, I'd guess not. You're pretty amazing though, you know that right."

"I'm just a woman trying to raise her son. Now, are we going to eat some pie or just stare at it?"

"Let's dig in. It's hard to pick a favorite, but I think this might be mine."

Chelsea grinned and took a bite. "Wow, definitely not disappointed."

"The spice kick is the best."

"I like the creaminess after."

Mick coughed and had to take a sip of his coffee to stop.

"You okay?" Chelsea placed her hand on his back.

Mick looked at her and smiled. "I'm good." He lifted his hand to her face and used his thumb to brush against her lip. "There, that's better."

Mick leaned toward Chelsea, and she leaned toward him.

Ding-dong.

Chelsea jumped back.

"Sorry. Let me get rid of whoever it is." Mick disappeared down the hall.

Chelsea touched her lips where Mick's hand had just been. *Stupid doorbell.*

"You ready to go? You don't look ready."

Chelsea recognized Duncan's voice. Of all the people in Anastasia, it had to be her brother-in-law at the door.

"Ready for what?"

"Shopping for the veteran's service day?" Duncan's voice grew louder. "Chelsea?"

"Hey Duncan." Chelsea stood and hugged him.

Duncan sees the pie and coffee on the island, "Sorry, am I interrupting something?"

Chelsea and Mick in unison, "No."

Duncan smirks.

"I'm on my way out, Eli needs a couple of things for his science project."

"Let me walk you to the door." Mick offered.

Chelsea nodded. "Later Duncan."

"Later."

Chelsea walked down the hall toward the front door. She didn't dare look at Mick, she was too embarrassed.

"I'm sorry Chelsea, I forgot about my plans with Duncan."

"You don't have anything to be sorry about, I surprised you."

"Yes, you did." Mick smiled.

Chelsea's knees wobbled a bit. "Um, well. Enjoy the rest of the pie. See you at practice."

"Maybe before practice?"

"See you at practice." Chelsea hurried out the door before anything else she'd regret could happen.

Mick watched Chelsea for a few seconds before he closed the door. He rested his forehead against the cool door. She did his heart good if only he could convince her. He turned and returned to the kitchen to find Duncan chowing down on a piece of the pie.

Duncan paused, and his eyes drilled into Mick. "What the heck are you doing? You are my best friend, but she's family. Alex will wring both our necks when you break her heart."

"Your neck will be fine. I'm not going to break her heart."

"You know what happened to her this year."

"I do, and for the last time I'm telling you, I will not break her heart." Mick took the empty plates and coffee cups and put them in the dishwasher.

"For both our sakes I hope you're right."

Chapter Six

♥

A WEEK AFTER ALMOST kissing Chelsea, a week of wishing he had kissed Chelsea, Mick looked down from the top of the ladder he climbed to get to the gutters on the house of one of the veterans on his group's list. He could see everyone in his group in the front yard, including Chelsea. He'd need to thank Duncan later because despite the reluctance Duncan voiced earlier, he'd assigned her to Mick's team.

Mick half-heartedly removed debris from the gutters while he watched Chelsea help some of the kids gather leaves into bags. Every so often a handful of leaves would go flying and Chelsea's laugh filled the air. Her laughter did something to him. He wasn't sure he liked it, but he didn't want it to stop either.

Mick was pleased when she let Eli stay back at the station. He'd seen it before when a kid got hurt, their mother would turn into a helicopter mom not allowing them out of their sight. It was nice to see Chelsea wasn't like that. Mick suggested it might be better if Eli sat this one out, he didn't mind being the bad guy. Eli was disappointed but didn't give Mick a hard time. The crew probably had him doing something, so he felt like he was contributing without all of us having to worry he'd further injure himself. Mick turned his full attention back to the gutters. They were a mess, at least this was the last run he'd have to clean out, the rest of the house was finished.

"Coach." Chelsea's voice drifted up to Mick. He took a deep breath before looking at her. "What's up?"

Chelsea shielded her eyes with her hand to block out the sun. "The guys are wondering if they can break for lunch."

Mick glanced over his shoulder, and the yard was completely void of leaves. Cleaning the gutters took longer than he anticipated. Looks like he chose the wrong chore. Mick smiled. "They did good work, I can't believe they're done already."

Chelsea grinned. "So, is that a yes?"

"Yes, thank you."

Chelsea nodded, then turned to the boys and gave them a thumbs up. They rushed around her and gave her a group hug. Too bad his phone was in the truck, that would have made a great picture. He turned back to the gutters, they wouldn't finish cleaning themselves.

"What can I do to help?" Chelsea's voice surprised Mick.

"You don't want to go with the boys?"

"Lunch with a group of mostly pre-teen boys? I think I'll pass." Chelsea chuckled.

"When you put it that way. I'm almost done, just need to rinse the gutters out. Could you hand me the hose?"

Chelsea picked it up and held it with its nozzle pointed toward him. "This hose?"

Her smile was somewhere between sweet and naughty. He was in so much trouble. "Yes, thanks. Mick held out his hand and hoped she'd hand it over.

Instead, she pushed the lever, and water sprayed but missed him. "Oops." She redirected it and pushed again, water misted over him.

"Funny."

"I think so." She lifted the nozzle as if to do it again.

"Don't."

"Don't?"

Mick started down the ladder.

Chelsea giggled.

Mick jumped down, skipping the last three rungs on the ladder.

Chelsea shrieked, pulled lightly on the nozzle, and water misted over Mick again.

Mick took a step toward her, and she turned to back out of his reach, but her feet got tangled in the hose, and she started to fall. Mick took an extra-long step and caught Chelsea. He turned her to face him and pulled her toward him. His lips were maybe a half inch from hers when Master Sergeant Miller called to them.

"I can't thank you, kids, enough for this. I wish I didn't need the help, to be honest."

Chelsea took a step back and seeing her blush was almost worth the interruption.

"We're glad to help. This isn't a one-time thing sir. We'll be back every couple of weeks to help with whatever you need." Mick offered as he turned to face the man.

"Aw now, that won't be necessary." Master Sergeant Miller protested.

"Well, then you can turn us away once we arrive. Deal?" Mick stuck his hand out for the master sergeant to shake.

He smiled and grabbed Mick's hand. "Deal."

When Mick turned to introduce Chelsea to the master sergeant, she was gone. Sneaky, sneaky, sneaky.

Chapter Seven

C HELSEA REPLAYED THE SOUND her car made right before it stalled. *Chit-chit-clunk.* It was the clunk that worried her the most. She'd called Alex for the save, and now all she could do was wait. The only bright side to be found was the family of deer playing in the field next to the road. If only happiness were that easy. She'd done everything she was supposed to do, hadn't she? Got good grades, went to a great college, occasionally went to church, met the alleged man of her dreams, and had a beautiful son. They should be dancing in the field. Instead, the offending man of her dreams broke her heart, she and her son were essentially homeless, and as of now, she was without a car.

"Well, at least it can't get any worse. Can I get an amen, deer family?" Chelsea watched as the three deer stopped what they were doing and darted into the tree line.

Chelsea shrugged then turned her attention back to the road and noticed a vehicle driving toward her. Please let it be Alex. Next time she broke down in the middle of nowhere you better bet she'd have a basket of books in the back seat. She had no use for boredom.

A Chevy Suburban sporting circa 1977 design and a 2018 racing stripe paint job stopped and the driver's window rolled down.

Son of a....

"For someone who claims she doesn't like to be rescued you seem to need more than your fair share." Mick's grin made Chelsea want to scream.

"Well, Mr. Full-of-Himself, I do not require a rescue today. I already called Alex, and she will be here soon."

Mick's smile grew wider, and the hair on Chelsea's neck danced in warning.

"I hate to break it to you, well, not really. I don't usually enjoy telling folks when they are mistaken, but today it doesn't seem so bad."

"What would that be?"

"Alex won't be arriving anytime soon, she called me and asked if I could come out to pick you up."

"No." *That traitor, she is so going to pay for this.*

"She did. I'll give you a lift, and we'll have Hank come out and tow that clunker of yours into the shop."

"I can't just leave her here." Chelsea's car had seen her through a category five divorce, a move cross country, and the loss of everything, except her son and his dog, in a house fire. The car was just as much a member of the family as any of them.

"Sure, you can, hell it'll be a miracle if anyone even drives by to see her."

Chelsea took a deep breath. He was right, damn it. No cars had gone by in the hour and a half she'd sat on the side of the road. Waiting for someone else to happen by wasn't exactly a winning strategy. Chelsea retrieved her purse from the back seat and joined Mick in his vehicle.

"Was that so hard?" Mick teased.

"Yes." Chelsea's voice carried her frustration. "But thank you just the same."

"Hold the phone, you even said thank you. I don't know if I can give you a lift now."

"What?" The pitch of Chelsea's voice was so high, she didn't even recognize it as her own.

"You're probably an imposter." Mick coughed, probably to hide a laugh.

Chelsea released her breath so forcefully that it sounded like a growl. "Funny."

Mick looked rattled and coughed to clear his throat. "I agree, although you might not see it, it is funny. Now tell me, how's Eli's wrist?"

"Fine."

"That's good."

"Yep."

"Will he have to do physical therapy?"

"No."

"How's your stay with Alex and Duncan?"

"Crowded." Couldn't he see she wasn't in the mood to chat? She shifted so she essentially turned half her back to him as she pretended to look out the window.

The five miles to Hank's shop went by slower than a turtle walking in peanut butter, but Mick finally pulled in front of Hank's shop.

"I'll wait and give you a lift to Magnolia."

"Thanks, but there's no need. I can walk from here." Chelsea picked up her purse and reached for the door handle.

"I don't mind, really."

"I appreciate it, but it isn't a problem. I can practically see Magnolia from here."

"If you're sure."

"I'm sure. Thanks for the lift."

"You're welcome, I'm accustomed to coming to the rescue." Mick winked at Chelsea.

"Impossible." Chelsea slid out of the vehicle. "You're completely impossible."

Chelsea closed the door and made her way inside.

Alex is in soooo much trouble when I see her. So much.

Thirty minutes later Alex slammed Magnolia Inn's front door. "Alex! Alexandra Marie Drake Cordova you better show yourself if you know what's good for you."

"Is there a problem sis?" Alex asked with a smirk.

"Don't you sis me, you traitor."

"I don't know what you're talking about, it would have taken me forever to round up Eli and get Ashley into the car. Calling Mick was a much quicker solution."

"I knew you'd have to do all those things when I called you. I didn't mind waiting."

"Well, maybe I didn't like the idea of you stranded on the side of the road, in the middle of nowhere for any longer than you really needed to be. Besides, you like him, but you refuse to acknowledge it, and it's driving me crazy."

"Oh yeah? Well, maybe I do like him. So what?!"

Alex smiled but didn't say anything.

"Stop smiling."

"You just admitted you like Mick." Alex continued to smile.

"I know what I said." Chelsea folded her arms against her chest.

"Explain to me like I'm five why me sending the hunk of a man you like to rescue you, is such a bad thing."

Chelsea walked into the adjacent room, plopped down into one of the chairs, and let out a big sigh. "I really have to explain it? Okay, here goes. I'm an almost thirty-year-old divorced mother of a young son, who only has a roof over her head because her sister took pity on her, and I have no idea what I want to do with the rest of my life. He's being pursued by almost every single woman in town limits and I wouldn't be surprised if there are some married women interested too, he is the fire captain and little league coach, and if that wasn't enough he is arguably the sexiest man in the county.

"I'm not going to say you haven't had an unfair share of trauma recently, but, you don't give yourself enough credit. Mick is a good guy, considering Duncan lives here too he may not be the sexiest man in the county, but he obviously likes kids or he wouldn't be a coach. I just want you to give him a chance, I think there's something there."

"You're just saying that because you're my sister."

Alex walked over to Chelsea, put her hands on Chelsea's shoulders to help her stand, and then gave her a hug. "Doesn't mean it's not true."

Chapter Eight

♥

CHELSEA CARRIED THE LAST of what she thought they'd need for the cookout that Coach was throwing for the team to celebrate the end of the season. The wagon Alex was letting her borrow was a perfect size and made it so the group could walk to the festivities instead of drive which would be a plus since parking was limited.

Chelsea made her way to the kitchen where Alex, Duncan, baby Ashley, and Eli had congregated. "Oh sure, now I find y'all when all of the work has been done."

"Sounds perfect to me." Duncan teased.

"Are we ready to head over?" Alex asked.

Chelsea nodded. "Let's get this over with."

"Come on mom, it's going to be fun."

(Maybe for you). "You're right, Eli. I think I'm just tired from loading the wagon."

"Can we bring Jake?" Eli bent down to pet his dog.

"I don't think that's such a good idea, bud. There are going to be a lot of people, it's not the best setup to take Jake, we'll do something with him tomorrow."

Eli nodded, jumped up, and headed for the door.

Chelsea shook her head and leaned over to whisper to Alex. "Now that the season was over he is finally excited about going to baseball. There's something wrong with this picture."

Alex laughed. "I wouldn't be too disappointed, I think he's more excited about the food than the baseball."

"That's true, I'm glad I've got you around to remind me of the important things." Chelsea smiled.

"That's what sisters are for."

They walked the rest of the way to the cookout in relative silence if you didn't count Eli singing the team's unofficial theme song.

When they arrived at the park Eli ran off to play with his friends, and Alex sent Duncan with Ashley to supervise.

Alex helped Chelsea set a table with their stuff and spread a blanket where the awards ceremony would be.

Chelsea saw an older woman with a cane dragging a lawn chair behind her so she turned to Alex, "I'll be right back."

Alex nodded.

Chelsea made her way to the woman. "Can I help?"

The woman smiled. "Only if we hurry so my daughter doesn't see. I just made a pretty big deal about doing it myself, but I got halfway across this dang field and regretted my decision."

"Understood, where would you like to go?"

The woman surveyed the area and pointed to where Minnie May, Miss Sadie, and Miss V sat. "There's good, I've been out of town and need to find out what's been going on around here."

Chelsea nodded, made her way to the trio, and set the chair next to Minnie May. If you're looking for gossip you might as well go directly to the queen bee.

The women paused their conversation and at first gave Chelsea a funny look.

"You're so wrapped up in whoever yer talkin' about that ya don't even know I'm here." The woman scolded.

"Cora!" The three chimed in unison.

"When did you get back?" Miss V asked.

Cora sat in her chair. "Not back, unfortunately, just visitin'. Tamika is keepin' me, prisoner."

"I'm sure she's ready for ya to head home as much as yer ready to be here." Miss Sadie joked.

"Enjoy your day." Chelsea nodded toward the ladies and then turned to go back to where she and Alex set up their table.

"You can count on it." Cora called after her.

While she walked back to the table she saw Mick. He and a couple of firemen she recognized were standing over one of the fire pits and it appeared like they were discussing the best way to stack the charcoal. Chelsea squinted to read the shirt Coach wore, Eat, Sleep, Baseball, Repeat. Seemed fitting.

Mick lifted his head, locked eyes on Chelsea, and smiled.

Chelsea waved, but kept her hand low, No need to draw attention to herself.

He did the same, but the firemen next to him saw it and looked in her direction. She could feel her cheeks burning and she hightailed it back to Alex.

"Subtle." Alex teased.

"Well, I tried to be."

"Incoming," Alex warned.

"Chelsea, we could use another hand with serving lunch. Would you help?" Keiko, an aunt to one of the players and a member of Minnie May's hive, asked.

"Sure, I can help."

"Great, follow me."

Chelsea followed Keiko to the buffet.

"Here's good. Thanks for the help."

"Sure, glad to." Chelsea took her position and watched Keiko walk by Miss Sadie and give her a high five. (That's odd).

"I think you've been trying to avoid me, all day." Mick's voice from behind Chelsea made her flinch.

"I haven't been thinking of you at all."

"Ouch."

"You seemed busy."

"So you have been paying attention to me."

"What? No, not exactly."

"I don't believe you."

Chelsea shrugged. "That's your prerogative."

Chelsea tried to pretend that being in his orbit didn't have any effect on her, but she wasn't sure she was convincing anyone. She definitely wasn't convincing herself. Slinging macaroni and cheese onto people's plates didn't help Chelsea forget Mick was standing next to her. *If you can beat them, join them.*

"So, Coach, what made you decide to be a coach?"

"Someone asked me." Mick didn't look at her, just continued to scoop baked beans on plates as people went through the line.

"Okay, sure, but if someone asked me I would have said no. Why did you say yes?"

"I hate to break it to you, but it was a simple because I could. I get to see a lot of kids in my line of work and usually not in the best of circumstances. I thought by becoming a coach I might be able to help some kids in a way that didn't include trauma and get some exercise that didn't feel like exercise."

"Seems reasonable. I have to say though, I am surprised you aren't married with a family. The ladies in town think highly of you and it's obvious you like kids."

"I think they are more enamored with the idea of dating a fireman and not the reality, besides until now I hadn't met anyone I was interested in enough to consider long-term."

"Oh." Chelsea didn't know what to say after that. Was he talking about her or someone else? She wasn't sure, but she didn't like the feeling she had when she decided he must be talking about someone else.

Duncan saved her by pulling Mick off the line to direct the volunteers on how to set up the awards table for the ceremony.

Chelsea finished helping with the food and then went to grab a glass of punch.

"You and my brother make a pretty good team." A woman who walked up to the punchbowl as Chelsea finished her glass said.

"What's that?" *Her brother?*

"My brother, Mick. You and he make a good team."

"I'm sorry, I don't know what you mean. We aren't a team."

"In the food line, you worked well together. I'm Tamika by the way."

"Oh, I guess we did. I'm Chelsea."

"Nice to meet you, any chance you could help me carry these? I don't seem to have enough hands." Tamika pointed to the glasses of punch she poured.

"Sure." Chelsea grabbed two of the glasses and followed Tamika.

"I see you've met my new friend," Cora said as Tamika handed her one of the glasses of punch.

Chelsea nodded to Cora, then handed a glass of punch to Miss Sadie and Miss V.

"Well now, isn't that interesting? Looks like you've met the whole family now." Tamika said as she handed Minnie May the last glass of punch.

Chelsea was super confused.

"This is Mick and my mama."

Chelsea could feel her eyes go wide. "Oh, ooooh."

"Is that a problem?" Cora asked.

"No ma'am. I just didn't realize." Chelsea tripped over her words.

"Didn't realize what?" Mick walked and stopped beside Chelsea.

"That Cora was your mom." Miss V offered.

"She helped me when I arrived." Cora nodded.

"Is that right? Well, I just saw you help my sister carry punch, my mama says you helped her earlier, so I only think it's fair you help me with the awards ceremony." Mick looked down at her and smiled.

"What? I'm sure there's someone better suited to help you than me." Chelsea rebuked.

"You know all of the boys and they know you, I think it is perfect." Mick's smile morphed into a smirk. "Let's go, we should get started."

Chelsea didn't move. She tried to come up with an excuse, any excuse to decline.

"Go on now." Miss Sadie encouraged.

Chelsea couldn't think fast enough to create a valid reason to back out and so she reluctantly followed Mick to the awards table.

Thirty minutes later they had made it to the last award. Chelsea was excited to be done and as soon as the last name was announced she and Eli would be hightailing it out of there. She could only people so much and today she had hit the limit too many hours ago.

"This last award is going to someone who worked really hard this season. He had a few hiccups and an injury but through it all he never gave up. This year's most improved player goes to Eli Drake."

Chelsea's heart felt like it would burst. Eli's face lit up like the Fourth of July. Eli ran to get his trophy from Mick and then stopped and gave Chelsea a hug before running back to his aunt. Chelsea turned away from Mick and the crowd so she could wipe away a tear or two. It had been such a difficult year, but seeing Eli so happy brought her an overabundance of joy.

Chapter Nine

♥

T HE SUN BURST THROUGH the café windows to light the entire café. Mick sat in a booth near the kitchen and surveyed his fellow diners. Happiness. That's the overwhelming feeling he felt as he looked around the café. He closed his eyes, inhaled deeply, and smiled while he exhaled. He'd always felt blessed to be a part of the community, and that feeling had only grown since he became Anastasia's fire captain.

Mick opened his eyes to find Eli walking quickly toward him. That kid's smile could melt the evil queen's heart. Chelsea stood at the door, with a less-than-pleased look. Mick would take the fifty percent win for now.

"Coach!"

"Eli, good to see you, my man!" Mick held up his hand to high five Eli and Eli didn't hold back.

"I secretly hoped you'd be here. Will you join us for lunch?" Eli asked.

Chelsea had made her way to stand behind Eli. She half-smiled. "I'm sure Coach has other places to be."

"As a matter of fact, I don't. I'd love to join you, actually, why don't you join me?" Mick gestured to the booth across from him.

Eli didn't look at Chelsea he just slid into the booth across from Mick. Chelsea was slow to follow but finally seemed to surrender and slid into the seat next to her son.

"Looks like your wrist is feeling better."

"It is. I think the doctor is going to release me so I can play at this week's game."

"That's great. Glad to hear it, I'm proud of how much you've improved Eli. You've done terrific."

"Thanks, Coach!"

Alex walked into the café and walked to the counter. "Hey Miss Sadie, I'm here for Duncan's order. Poor guy is working so hard he won't even take a break for lunch."

"Sounds like him. It's almost ready, why don't ya take a seat on that stool right there." Miss Sadie smiled and took a glass from the counter to fill with ice water.

Alex took a seat and noticed her sister in the corner of the café. "Well, would you look at that. Their auras match."

Miss Sadie dropped the water glass she had in her hand. "Oh mercy. What a mess. What was that you said, Alex?"

"Nothing important really, I just said their auras match."

Miss Sadie coughed, then asked. "You see auras?"

"Don't be such a skeptic. I see auras, at least that's what I'm calling them. Auras are...."

"I know what an aura is dear. I'm surprised because I didn't know ya could see them."

"I think I could as a kid but then stopped for some reason. When I got pregnant with Ashley, I started seeing them, and over the past few months they've gotten brighter."

"Is that right?" Miss Sadie's voice barely above a whisper.

"It is, I stopped questioning it. I don't often see matching auras though."

Miss Sadie slowly nodded. Alex couldn't blame her if she weren't the one seeing the auras she'd have a hard time believing it herself.

"Well, we should probably get this to Duncan before he sends out a search party. Got to love the man, even if he is more than a bit overprotective."

"Ya best be givin' me a hug before you hightail it out of here."

Miss Sadie walked around the counter, hugged Alex, and then watched her head out of the cafe. Seeing her filled her heart unlike almost anything else. Alex can see auras. Miss Sadie had known a few people during her extended life who could see them, so it wasn't completely unheard of, but Alex always seemed a bit different. Throw in that Ashley was able to change grandmother's staff into a rattle and the way her eyes sparkled that day. Miss Sadie shook her head in confusion and returned to work behind the counter. *Don't be silly, let's get back to work.*

The kids took the field, and Mick stood next to the chain link fence. He tried and failed to pretend Chelsea wasn't there. She was a distraction of the best kind. The team had improved enough he didn't have to watch them so closely. It had its pros and cons. If he weren't careful the hive, Anastasia's gossip corps would go into overdrive. He didn't need that kind of scrutiny right now. Well, he never liked that kind of examination of his private life, as fire chief, he'd just come to expect it.

He'd dated his fair share but more recently decided to take a break. He wanted to settle down and have a family, but most of the ladies he knew were obsessed with the fantasy of a firefighter but not the reality. The always being on call, no matter the premade plans. BBQ or birthday party or even Christmas had the chance to be interrupted by work. He didn't drink for fear of being called in and not being able to go on a call with his men.

Screams from the field drew Mick back to the present. Just in time to see his team make a double play. A few more of those and they'd end up in the championship. Who would have thought a few weeks ago that would be on their radar? These kids had done a lot of work.

The rest of the game went about the same and the team easily won.

"Congrats Coach." Hannah offered.

Mick was pretty sure he saw Chelsea roll her eyes. His smile was for her, but he guessed she thought it was for Hannah. Too bad.

"Thank you but the boys did all the work. I just stood back and let them do their thing."

"My nephew thinks you walk on water. I'm inclined to agree."

"Like I said, it's the boys. Hey, Chelsea do you have a minute?"

Chelsea snapped her head up and nodded. She was so damn cute when she was confused.

"Okay, bye." Hannah and her nephew left.

"What can I do for you Coach?" Chelsea's emphasis on the word coach bugged Mick.

"Nothing. You just did it. Sorry I resorted to using you."

Chelsea mumbled something.

"What?"

"Anytime."

Eli ran over. "Hey, Coach. I've got a play at school Thursday night, can you come?"

"Eli, I'm sure Coach has things he needs to do, and your play isn't one of them."

"Actually, I'd love to come to your play."

"You would?" Chelsea and Eli asked in unison.

Mick smiled. "Heck yeah."

"Awesome! It's at seven at the elementary school. I have the lead."

"Too cool. Can't wait." Mick reached over and tousled Eli's hair.

"Eli, could you take the bat bag to Coach's car. We'll catch up."

"Sure." Eli took the bag and headed toward the parking lot.

Chelsea waited for Eli to be out of earshot. "You don't have to come, really it's okay."

"I know, but I'll be there. Eli's a good kid, I don't mind. Besides, it will give me a chance to see his mom too."

Chelsea's cheeks turned red, and Mick smiled. He liked having an effect on her.

"Right. Sure. Okay. So, we'll see you on Thursday." Chelsea offered.

"See you then."

Mick watched her walk away and wished she was still standing next to him. What would he need to do to convince her to spend more time with him?

Chapter Ten

♥

C HELSEA AND ELI WALKED toward the Magnolia Inn from the elementary school. The night was a little chilly, but after spending a couple of hours in the stuffy school auditorium, the air felt good.

"I understand Auntie had to watch the inn with Uncle Duncan out of town, but I thought Coach would show." Eli kicked a stone from the sidewalk into the road.

"Me too, and I'm sorry he didn't." Chelsea tried to keep her voice calm, for Eli's sake. When she saw Mick next time, calm would be the furthest thing from her mind.

"I don't want to talk about it." Eli's voice was barely above a whisper.

"Okay. Auntie said she had a special treat for you since she couldn't make it. What do you think it is?"

"I don't know." Eli stared blankly into space as they walked.

Chelsea couldn't believe Mick's nerve. If he didn't want to come to the play, he could've said he had other plans. Eli didn't need another man in his life who refused to follow through on his promises.

This was precisely why she wouldn't date until Eli was off to college. She could hardly handle the rejection, how was Eli expected to understand sometimes things don't work out the way we hoped? He was learning too many adult lessons too soon, no need to do anything that magnifies that reality so young.

They walked up the drive to Magnolia Inn. If nothing else her sister had lucked out. Magnolia was gorgeous inside and out, and Duncan was too.

Chelsea and Eli made their way into the foyer, and Alex joined them from the parlor. Alex's expression flashed with what seemed to be confusion before she leaned over to Eli and whispered something Chelsea couldn't hear. The next moment Eli smiled and ran toward the kitchen.

"I can't believe he didn't show. I mean seriously? What a jerk. All he had to say was that he had other commitments tonight when Eli asked him. That's it, but noooo he goes and promises Eli he'll be there. Then he doesn't show. He's not going to like it when I see him next time, I can tell you that. Duncan might want to warn him. Better yet, no, he doesn't deserve a warning."

"Chelsea...."

"I'm serious, forget...."

"Chelsea...."

"I'm not...."

"Chelsea!"

"What?"

"I've been trying to call you." If Alex's forehead scrunched any more, her eyebrows would have touched.

"I turned my phone off after I got a picture of Eli on stage and I didn't want a text from that louse to ruin the show for me."

"Alex, what are you talking about?"

Alex scanned the room, "here, sit."

"I don't want to sit. I'm pissed, hello!"

"Trust me."

Chelsea made her way to the chair next to the front desk. "Happy now?"

"Chelsea, I'm surprised you're here because I thought you'd have listened to your voicemail, and be at the hospital."

"Why would I be at the hospital? You're not making a lick of sense."

"Chelsea. Mick's in the hospital."

"What? No, he skipped Eli's play."

"No, well he did, but not by choice. He was out on a call, and there was an accident."

Chelsea's body went numb. Her hand hit the chair, and she jumped up. "Is he, oh my God, What? I have to, what?

Alex's hand gripped Chelsea's arm. "They think he's going to be okay."

"They think? They think! There's a chance. No. I have to go."

"You're not going anywhere by yourself. Let me ask Stacy to watch Eli and Ashley, and I'll drive you. Duncan's be there by the time we arrive."

Chelsea sunk back into the chair and nodded.

It seemed like forever to get to the hospital. Chelsea weaved through the hospital hallways. Alex was there with her but her presence barely registered. She had to get to Mick. She had to apologize. She had to be sure he was going to be okay. Chelsea approached his room, Duncan was pacing outside. *Why isn't he in with Mick? No. No. No.*

Duncan stopped pacing and looked up at Chelsea and Alex.

"Why aren't you in there with him?"

"The nurse asked me to step out while she tended to him."

The nurse came out of the room.

"Can I see him?" Chelsea asked.

"Are you *family?*"

"Why?" He's...."

"His sister." Duncan blurts out.

Chelsea snaps her head toward Duncan. *Sister?*

"Right. Do I look like an idiot? Wait. Don't answer that. You're lucky it's a full moon, and mercury is in retrograde. I'm tired. You've got fifteen minutes, but that's it for everybody tonight. Got it?" The nurse's eyes burned a hole into Chelsea.

"Yes. Thank you." Chelsea inhaled. The antiseptic smell of the hospital burned her nose. She shook her head to banish the tears that threatened. The sight of him on the bed, unconscious, wires going every which way was almost more than she could take.

Chelsea pulled the chair from under the window to be closer to his bed. She took his hand and put her forehead to it. It didn't even smell like him. *Wait, when did she figure out what he smelled like?*

"I don't know if you can hear me, but I'm so sorry. I'm sorry I was mad at you, I'm sorry for calling you names under my breath when I figured out you weren't going to show." Chelsea took a deep breath and kissed the back of his hand. "I'm sorry for immediately thinking you were just like every other man in Eli's life and thinking that you chose to let him down rather than show up. I'm sorry I didn't tell you I think I'm falling in love with you. I do. God, please let you be okay."

"Are you going to stop talking and kiss me or what?" Mick's voice was quiet but had a bit of a teasing note to it.

"What? I mean. How much did you hear?"

Mick smiled. "That's not important. Kiss me, Chelsea."

"I...."

"Please don't make me sit up." Mick winked.

Chelsea stood and leaned in and kissed him.

His heart rate monitor beeped and made them both jump.

"You better calm down, or we're both going to hear it from your nurse." Chelsea grinned.

"Worth it." Mick laughed and then grabbed his side.

"Sorry."

"Stop saying that. I think I love you, Chelsea Drake."

"And, God help me, I think I love you, Mick Wilson."

"Good. Move in with me."

"What?"

"You and Eli should move in with me."

"I don't know."

"Yes, you do."

Chelsea searched Mick's eyes. He was right, this muscular huggable unshakable man was correct, she did know. She nodded and leaned in for another kiss.

Recipe

❤

O ATMEAL CINNAMON PIE

Crust:

1 Cup Flour

1 Cup (Ground) Oats

¼ Cup Brown Sugar (lightly packed)

1 Stick Butter, melted + about a tablespoon unmelted butter to grease the pie pan

1 tablespoon vanilla extract

1 tablespoon water

Filling:

8 ounces cream cheese, softened

1 Cup brown sugar, packed

2 large eggs plus 1 egg yolk

1 ¼ Cups heavy cream

¼ cup all purpose flour

6 ½ tablespoons ground cinnamon

2 teaspoons vanilla extract

1 teaspoon salt

Directions:

Crust -

1. Preheat oven to 375 degrees.

2. Put oats into a food processor and grind into a coarse grind. The ground oats should equal 1 cup.

3. Whisk together flour and oats.

4. Stir in the brown sugar, melted butter, vanilla extract, and water until just blended.

5. Grease the bottom and sides of a 9-inch pie pan with unmelted butter. Then press the crust into the bottom and sides of the pan, using your fingers.

6. Bake for 10-13 minutes.

Filling:

7. Adjust oven to 350 degrees.

8. In the bowl of an electric mixer. Beat the cream cheese and brown sugar until light and fluffy, about 3 – 5 minutes.

9. Scrape the bowl then beat in the eggs. Scrape the bowl again, then on low, mix in cream, flour, cinnamon, vanilla, and salt until very smooth.

10. Pour the mixture into the crust.

11. Bake for 35 minutes, until the center seems set when jiggled, but not totally firm. Bake another 5 minutes if needed.

12. Cool completely. Cover and chill. Take out of the refrigerator 1 hour before serving. Dust the top with powdered sugar. Cut and serve with whipped cream if desired.

B ELOW YOU WILL FIND the current start to the eighth romance for the Flower Moon Café Series. Please note it is unedited and is subject to change. Enjoy!

<u>Sugar</u>

Where the heck is this place? Jen Everhart looked down at her phone screen just as it went blank. *Figures.* She had a charging cable, somewhere in the mess of bags and a few boxes, but as per usual, she didn't have a clue which one had what she needed. One of these days, she'd figure out how to keep tabs on the important things, but until then, she'd live without necessities like GPS on a back-country road.

She tossed the phone into the passenger seat and focused on the void in front of her. Her surroundings were foreign. She hadn't been out of the city for years, and the darkness of the road she found herself traveling, gave her an uneasy feeling. It was entirely possible the unease was rooted in the fact she'd left everyone and everything she'd ever known after signing a lease for a storefront in a town she'd never heard of until three days ago, no, nope, nada, it was most definitely the road. In her head, she knew there wasn't supposed to be another turn after the fork in the road, but her anxiety plucked at her like a pigeon searching for seeds in the grass. All she could do was hope for the best. If she were lost, it wouldn't be the first time she slept in her car.

When she left Atlanta, she thought she could get to Anastasia before dark, but apparently, she'd miscalculated. This wasn't an omen, just an unwelcome reminder she sucked at math. Once she got to Anastasia, things would fall into place if for no other reason than they had to. She turned the radio on, maybe a little music might help, but when Hank William's "Lost Highway" began to play, she turned it off. The universe must think it's a hoot, she wasn't amused.

A few minutes of silence passed when a glow began to emanate from the night, and as she followed the curve of the road, she unexpectedly found herself on Main Street in Anastasia. The town just kind of appeared out of nothingness. A wooden sign on the side of the road stated, "Welcome to Anastasia, a little slice of paradise" the sign indicated Magnolia Inn donated it.

The realtor, Hannah, had mentioned the inn, but she wouldn't be able to stay there. Every penny she had was for the bakery. The pennies were already spent or were about to be. She inched along Main Street, looking for numbers on the buildings. The little town was as quaint as she'd hoped. Idyllic even. Her anxiety quieted, maybe she'd finally found the place she belonged or at least someplace that won't cast her out at the first opportunity. Not that she cared what anyone else thought of her. They could all pound sand. She figured out a way to do the thing she loved, and no one would stop her.

2010 Main Street, there it was, the place that would be her universe. Her home, her business, her heart, and her soul. She parked and looked around, the streets were deserted, but there was a light on above Flower Moon Café. That it was the only sign of life was not at all surprising, restaurant owners were typically the first to rise and the last to sleep.

She took a deep breath. Freezer paper. Covering the windows should be the first order of business. She was too easily distracted, and if she tried to do something else first, she wouldn't get the windows covered before someone noticed her. Not at all what she wanted. Jen desired to create mystery and buzz. She doubted a town Anastasia's size had many mysteries. She might have always lived in cities, but she'd read enough books and watched enough holiday movies to know small towns had few secrets. She popped the trunk, and a mere twenty minutes later, she put her hands on the freezer paper, scissors, and tape she'd packed.

It took three runs to determine the best way to cover the windows. If someone else had been there, it would have gone quicker with fewer ups and downs on the chair serendipitously left by the previous owner, but it was what it was. She was pleased no one walked by, the vision she'd conjured as a plan seemed to hold.

Once the windows were covered, five trips from the car were all it took to ferry all her worldly possessions into the bakery. It seemed like there should be more. Jen shook it off and surveyed the inside of the building that would become *her* bakery, it looked more like a defunct boutique. Racks and hangers were everywhere without a table or food display case in sight. Where was Joanna Gaines when you needed her?

She moved the racks to the back instead of throwing them into the dumpster, maybe she could sell them. She found a wooden box and threw the derelict hangers in, and once they were all sequestered, she had to slide the box to the back because it was too heavy to lift. Who knew a few plastic hangers weighed more than a baby elephant? Everything was dusty, but exhaustion began to weave its way into her bones. She grabbed a broom and swept the floor. The dust everywhere else could wait until tomorrow.

She wanted to sketch the kitchen layout, but her brain begged for mercy. The drive took more out of her than she anticipated, or maybe it was knowing she was all alone in this world, again. It had happened enough. She should be used to it by now. Things had never been easy, but situations had been predictable. This, whatever this was, was about as far from predictable as she could get. She laid out her sleeping bag, and when she snuggled inside, she smiled. She'd slept in worse places. It was a blessing Marie came along when she did, or things might not have turned out as nicely. Was it too much to hope that for once, things seemed to be going her way?

About Author – April Alieda

April Alieda writes magical and mystical romance. If you've read her Flower Moon Cafe series, you'd never guess she has a serious love of cursing but that pairs well with her other love – Jameson Whiskey! She's a Disney villains and princesses fanatic and admits she's passionate about making the world a better place one story at a time.

She currently lives in Florida with her spouse and is blessed his three sons have welcomed her into their lives with open arms.

Please visit www.aprilalieda.com or my Amazon Author Page for updates on new releases and to see what I'm up to on a daily basis you can find me on Facebook, Instagram, Pinterest, and Twitter

Also By - April Alieda

♥

<u>Flower Moon Cafe Series</u>

All Who Wander

Citadel of the Heart

Unfinished Business

Getting Lucky in Love

X Marks the Heart

Devil's in the Details

On Fire

Sugar

Butterfly Blues
Evergreen Dreams

Stand Alone Stories

Christmas Temptation
Roses Ever After

Made in the USA
Columbia, SC
30 October 2022

70231466R00043